BLUE INK 2025

BLUE INK 2025

NORTHERN WRITERS

CONTENTS

Foreword	1
You Bleed through Your Tongue by Alicia Vargas	3
Wings of Wax by Tejasvi Annadurai	4
The Static Mind by Charles Beaudry	8
See You Again by Anthony Wells	10
The Victims of Time by Kuek Kuot	11
A Thousand Suns Slamming into Us by Rowan Fogg	12
Natant by Ava Czygan	13
Victims of Time by Morgan DeVries	15
Winter in Retreat by Rowan Fogg	16
Victim of the System by Anthony Wells	17
Ladybugs by Tara Peterson	20
Potato Beetle by Tara Peterson	21
Their Village by Adactreus	22
What Is Love by Alistar Meier	23
Revere by Jesse Liu	27
Evil Thoughts (excerpt) by Shi	28
Untitled by Ava Czygan	29
Shisif by Shi	30

The Island's Survivors by Charles Beaudry	31
Souleater by Morgan DeVries	34
Abstinence of Failure by Norhan Hassan	35
Eggs Are Nice by Alistar Meier	41
Prayers by Alicia Vargas Gonzalez	43
All Bark No Bite (excerpt) by Brooke Gordon	44
Subspace by Claire Newell	47
The Night Air Is Screaming at Us	48
Beauty in Plain Sight by Charles Beaudry	51
Dead Men by Adactreus	53
What It Means To Be Human by Tejasvi Annadurai	54

Foreword

In his revolutionary work *Republic*, Plato presents the allegory of the cave to explain what truth might mean for an individual and for the collective. Plato builds a scenario in which life-long prisoners in a cave are chained, facing a wall upon which others in the cave cast shadows. Not able to turn around and see that these shadows are coming from other people moving about and carrying different objects, the prisoners begin to believe that the shadows themselves are alive. They believe the living shadows are real, and build their sense of truth around the shadows, only able to understand the world through this lens. Truth, it seems, is what makes the most sense to us given what we know; how we navigate a changing world impacts what we hold to be true.

In this, the 11th edition of Blue Ink – the *Truth* edition – the writers of the Northern Writers' Club find meaning as they perceive the world around them. The works in this anthology organically came together around this theme, and the writers and artists between the covers present to you a number of unique ways to see the world around them.

In "The Island's Survivors," Charles Beaudry's protagonist gains his freedom, but quickly discovered that the safety he initially found in others was not, in fact, as true of a bet as he hoped. In "Souleater," Morgan DeVries shares commentary on how society's expectations and social media obscure the realities that women experience today. She writes, "If we can't even see ourselves as beautiful, how are we supposed to find the beauty in anything?" The poet Tejasvi Annadurai shares in "What It Means To Be Human" her perspective on life as continual wonder, finding her truth in a life lived in the present.

Back in the cave, Plato theorizes a time when the prisoners finally can break their chains to escape the cave and discover the truth of the world beyond the shadows on the wall. Some choose to be bold, break free, and find the true realities of life – that what they believed to be true was, in fact, an illusion. Others choose to stay in the cave, fearing the unknown or possibly learning that their perception of reality was false. The Northern Writers continue to escape their caves as they hear each other's voices week after week, taking in others perspectives and exploring the craft of writing.

This year, the Northern Writers has expanded its scope significantly welcoming many new creatives to our collective. Thank you to the wonderful leadership provided by our club leaders like Norhan Hassan for your vision. We continue to be a welcoming place for all writers and creatives to find their truths as they go forward in life. As poet Kuek Kuot shares in "The Victims of Time," we all can fall victim to time, in which "you become trapped, hemmed into your old ways of your past self / Until you are nothing."

The Northern Writers are *something*, and I invite you to discover their truths in this edition of *Blue Ink*.

Sean Duffie
Northern Writers' Club Advisor
(2012 -)

You Bleed through Your Tongue
by Alicia Vargas

You bleed through your tongue, despite all the wounds you have healed one has yet to fully close. Stitches, band-aids, needles through your lips won't help because the blood seeps through the cracks.

Your words spill out like a scarlet river, so clear, so raw.

You can't help that the hurt so etched into your very being, carved into your veins, slips out.

I know you don't mean it, it comes up your throat painting everything in red, your teeth no longer white now stained with emotion.

Yet it still smudges everything around you.

You bleed through your tongue, you can taste the tangy iron, food doesn't taste good anymore, it tastes like everything else. A gross iron.

How come everything else has healed, yet your tongue remains coated in a violent color.

People often mistake pain as intention, intention to hurt. Just because you can't taste anything but the crimson liquid doesn't mean everyone else is the same, and when you feel other lips cloying at yours, a foreign tongue slipping through your teeth, you'll know the moment they taste your sour scars.

You'll know in the way they recoil, in the way their expression contorts because you've let the blood seep through. You bleed through your tongue, and it stains everyone around you

Wings of Wax by Tejasvi Annadurai

They warned me,
    Don't fly too high.
        The sun isn't kind to dreamers.
But how could I resist,
when the sky called my name
like a mother searching for her lost child,
when the clouds whispered
that they had been waiting for me?
I didn't build my wings to defy gravity.
I built them to escape.
Escape the earth,
where every step felt like a shackle,
where every breath was a war against the weight
of expectations that weren't mine to carry.
So I tore feathers from the ribs of my dreams,
stitched them together
with threads of stubborn hope,
and dipped them in wax—
because I thought wax was strong enough
to hold me together.
I thought I was strong enough
to hold me together.
When I leapt,
the world fell away,
and for the first time,
I wasn't afraid.
The wind wasn't just air;
it was freedom,
it was forgiveness.
The sky wasn't just blue;
it was a canvas,
splattered with my defiance.
The sun

oh, the sun.
It wasn't just light—
it was a lover,
blinding and burning,
pulling me closer with every heartbeat.
I thought I could trust it.
I thought it would understand
that I didn't want to steal its throne—
I only wanted to dance in its glow.
But the sun is a jealous god.
It sees ambition as arrogance,
wings as rebellion,
and wax as weakness.
It touched me,
softly at first,
then all at once,
and my wings began to bleed.
The feathers screamed as they unraveled.
The wax wept as it melted into my skin,
dripping like promises
I couldn't keep to myself.
The wind turned cruel,
a thief in the night,
stealing my balance,
my courage,
my everything.
And then I fell.
The ground rushed toward me
like it had been waiting,
like it had always known
I'd come crawling back.
My body hit the earth
with the sound of shattering glass,
and my heart—
my foolish, hopeful heart—
broke open.
They all saw the fall.
They pointed,
whispered,
laughed.
We told you so, they said.

You should've stayed where it was safe.
But safety is a cage,
and I was born to fly.
You don't understand what it means
to be pulled upward by a dream
so fierce it feels like a command.
To stretch your hands toward the horizon
even when you know
it might destroy you.
And yes, I fell.
Yes, my wings turned to ash.
Yes, the ocean swallowed me whole,
and for a moment,
I thought it would keep me there.
But even broken,
I am a phoenix.
Even drowning,
I am a storm.
Because the truth is,
I touched the sky.
I danced with the sun.
I kissed the stars,
and they kissed me back.
For a fleeting, blazing moment,
I was infinite.
So let them call me reckless.
Let them call me foolish.
Let them believe that falling
means failing.
I will gather the feathers again.
I will find stronger wax.
And I will rise.
Because I
Because I
would rather break a thousand times
than spend a single lifetime
with my feet chained to the ground.
Because the fall isn't the end—
it's the beginning.
The cracks in my skin
are maps of the skies I've touched.

The scars on my hands
are constellations of courage.
And the ocean that tried to claim me?
It couldn't extinguish the fire in my chest.
They don't tell you this about falling:
You don't just plummet into darkness.
You fall into truth.
Into yourself.
And when you hit the earth,
when you shatter,
you find the pieces of you
that are unbreakable.
Icarus wasn't a tragedy.
He was a revelation.
Proof that we are meant to burn,
to risk,
to hurt,
to rise.
That the pain of the fall
is worth the glory of the flight.
So I will climb again.
Higher this time.
I will not be afraid of the sun.
It cannot destroy me.
It only makes me brighter.
And one day,
when they see me soaring—
my wings stronger,
my heart braver—
they will finally understand:
Wings of wax
were never meant to last,
but the soul behind them?
That's eternal.

The Static Mind by Charles Beaudry

July 23rd, 2024

I can't believe it's almost midnight, I haven't even done anything useful today. All I've done is get ready for the morning and then lie in bed all day. I don't even know why I got dressed, I haven't gone outside once. Well, actually, I have. I got the mail from my mailbox today. I don't know if that makes it better or worse.

Okay, I need to focus on what's been on my mind all day, my phone. I've been on my phone nonstop, and my eyes are strained from the screen being so close to my face. I don't need to check in a mirror to know my eyes are red, nor do I want to. I can only blame myself for being so lazy, lying in bed, scrolling through TikTok and Twitter. I don't even think I've eaten yet today. Have I? I don't know why I can't remember. It isn't because I've practically melted my brain looking at my screen, right?

Every time I write, I see my terrible handwriting, which is why I don't write in this journal anymore. I never had a good education, only because we live in such a run-down part of the state. My mom never had enough money to get us out of here. Despite it all, I still write. I still write because I need to go back to my journal to give myself the strength to improve myself. I need to give myself the strength to go outside, even when danger is around every corner, the strength to go on, and the strength to get off my phone for once!

The truth is, I can't escape from my phone even as I'm writing this. There's a video playing on my phone to act as background noise. I haven't listened to anything the guy has rambled about during the video. I'm not yet at the stage where I can do anything without my phone playing a video. I don't even know why I have it on, I'm going to turn it off...as soon as I finish writing, I swear.

I just don't want to be glued to my phone, day after day, but I can't help it. I should've read the terms and conditions of all the apps I've dedicated my life to. I think there was a condition saying that the companies could keep a chain around my neck and arms, pulling me back into the old habit of scrolling. I'm held prisoner as the videos are amplified, my brain full of static and my phone scorching hot for being used so long that it burns my hand.

I'm smiling in front of everyone, playing an act as people watch my videos. Behind the curtains, I'm screaming, yet no noise comes out. I'm at the bottom of the ocean as I struggle to breathe, yet I stay invested in these videos. I reach for the light outside of the screen, but as it gets darker, I'm dragged deeper down, and it all restarts, the cycle repeating again and again. When will it end?

I don't even know why I'm complaining so much. I did this to myself when I installed all those apps, and now I feel like puking if I keep looking back up at my screen. Why don't I just shut off my phone now? God, I'm so stupid. I don't know how much I can write anymore. My hand is on fire, and I fear it will fall off if I continue writing.

Whatever, I guess I can't escape from it. I signed a contract and sold my soul. I sold my soul to a phone. I'm done trying to fight it, it hurts when I do. It hurts when I can't see those bright, vibrant colors on my screen and rot away in bed. I'm so stupid, I drank the poison I poured myself. Still, I wonder why I feel so sick.

See You Again by Anthony Wells

The Victims of Time by Kuek Kuot

1 " لوقت كالسيف إن لم تقطعه قطعك "
(al-waqtu kassaif in lam takta hu qata'ak)

    There will come a darkness
Where radiance is most coveted
Where hope and justice are no longer prevailing
Where cities, towns, and villages are fragmented
What remains is little
Those who fall victim to time
To the past
It's a dangerous, murderous feeling
It isn't safe
It blinds you, altering your thoughts and feelings
You become someone else, a carbon copy of who you were and who you could be
It'll blind you before it kills you
You become trapped, hemmed into your old ways of your past self
Until you are nothing
Nothing without your melancholia
And then,
Then, you are just like them
You are the darkness

A Thousand Suns Slamming into Us by Rowan Fogg

The birds of false purity are coming in force this season
Just last week we had nine flocks
Not small ones either
Their legions made the night radiant
Like a thousand suns slamming into us
We beat them back though
We always do
However many ash bullets, argus blades, thorn bound contracts, and heroic sacrifices it takes
We'll live long enough to gain scars
Long enough to see our children go from catching soul worms to swinging through the arterial jungles and taking bone rafts fishing on the reefs of pale hands
Our world is a tapestry of scars old and new
The air trembles with the echos of their songs
To the sea, to the sea!
I'll kill you! I'll kill you all!
A double order of chicken wraps with a side of fries
They mock us, even through slit throats
Their feathers fall white and brilliant
Incendiary
The flames of false purity leave not even ashes
Their blood vaporizes to rust colored clouds
That dull red consumes our sky
Their bones litter our borders, metallic and white hot for decades
Our skirmishes rage for centuries
It matters not
We will grieve, we will kill, we will die,
Forever
The next one is coming
Ready your weapon

Natant by Ava Czygan

Victims of Time by Morgan DeVries

The old man of time sits by the sea watching the rocks erode. "What will come of any of us." you ask.

The man smiles as he talks. "You may not live after this moment, or you could live to 100. Nothing will stay the same, forests will burn and regrow, cities will turn to dust, and these rocks will have become sand. The inability to tell how things will go is truly frightening isn't it my child." but the next words he said are what truly made me think. " The only thing worth considering when thinking about tomorrow is if you would feel accomplished dying today. If yes, try to feel even more so, and if not, try your hardest, because even trying is daunting."

At the end of the day you can either be a victim of time, or its friend. What you need to do is decide which one. Live your life to the fullest so when it's your time you can confidently be ready and willing to go.

Winter in Retreat by Rowan Fogg

That hollow melancholy of waning winter

    Walking to school under a sky like a blue light filter

  A painter's depressed phase

Snow in retreat

ceding to wet pavement and cropped grass

Crunch of thin ice under your boots

In tendrils of creeping green

Spring arrives

Victim of the System by Anthony Wells

Sam, she was coming to realize, was not just *Sam.*

It had become increasingly obvious that this was not the case. This had never been the case. Sam was not just Sam, and Sam, no matter how lonely she always found herself feeling, was never truly alone in her body- Her body, which was not quite hers to begin with.

Perhaps it had started with the cat.

He'd always had his oddities- Damien had never been the most normal of companions. Sometimes, he was incredibly sweet to her- nuzzling into her leg and seeking out attention with the familiarity of a cat and its owner. But, of course, then there were other instances- The times when Sam would come home and Damien would keep a significant distance, and sometimes even hiss at her when she set her keys down in front of the entryway mirror that always greeted her upon her return. Damien had never liked that mirror. And, when she really thought about it, Sam didn't either. It had a gloomy air to it, and the rusted silver outline offered an oddly warped perception of her reflection.

Today had been one of *those* days, when the mirror's unsettling air was a bit harder to shake off than normal, and Damien had let out an awful shrill of a hiss upon her arrival.

"Damien?" She'd asked, crouching down to the floor and extending one hand out to him. "What's wrong? It's only me." The cat only stared, so still he might as well have been a statue. Nothing. No response.

Sam was tempted to just ignore it. Damien was a *cat,* after all, and so many people had reminded her what fickle beings cat's were- but he was almost never *this* far on edge. He had his bad days, and, lately, it had become even more common for him to react to her like this, but regardless, it remained positively unnerving. His voice wasn't usually that high pitched and raspy. He sounded rather upset indeed, and Sam was sure it had something to do with that damned mirror.

She stood up, and stared into her reflection in the mirror, which she was now noticing almost seemed a darker tint than usual. Her reflection looked like her, at least; Shaggy, unkempt brown hair that hadn't been properly washed in days, dark circles outlining the bottom crease of her eyes, and a faded scar under her right eye that she had woken up with one day and lived with ever since. She never *did* find out where it came from, but it was there, and as far as she knew, it was hers. It was certainly her face, at least, her body- but not quite her, either. Her reflections had always felt off. This was always how it was, and she'd convinced herself it was normal, but some part of her was fully aware that it most definitely was *not*, and that part of her hated that feeling- That feeling that the body she was in wasn't quite hers.

"Damien," She called, her own voice a tad raspier than normal- not that she could make it out all that well, with nothing more than a murmur reaching her ears. "I don't think this is normal."

No response.

She stepped closer to her mirror, and it stared back with such a daunting air about it, almost taunting her, that she felt short of breath. It was at that point when she realized bruises on her neck, and a slight gasp slipped past her lips. By now she'd grown used to finding bruises and cuts all over herself that she didn't recognize. It was like little clues left behind for her to unravel, little mysteries on her *own body*. Sometimes, they seemed rather intentional, like they were left only to confuse her, or to ensure that she spent her days unrelentingly followed by the dull ache of purple bruised into her skin. However, this time, It looked like she had been choked, and no matter how accustomed she might have been to inexplicable bruises, choking was most certainly a way to kill someone, as far as she could remember- At least, choking significant enough to leave skin in such a state.

She felt a bit faint when she finally stepped back. Choking marks, on her own body, and she had no idea where they'd come from. Surely, she'd have remembered if someone tried to *kill* her?

She stood there for a moment, letting the shock soak into her bones, still in her disheveled work clothes, with one shoe on and the other a few feet away from flicking it off as soon as she'd come home. And she stayed there for a moment, until her thoughts caught up to her, and it was as if up until that moment she truly had been killed and dead. She had already begun stumbling hazedly into the kitchen by the time she *realized* she was running, her body still caught far behind her mind.

The dining table was long, stretching down the entirety of the somber, empty dining room, draped in white cloth, decorated by tear stains and rips in the lace that lined the edges. It was exactly the sort of table you'd expect to see in a house like hers, and the old, victorian-style architecture of it all was very fitting for the ever-increasing disturbed aura of the evening. At the end of the aged table, which, empty and tired, looked almost a mile long, was a piece of paper. It shouldn't have been there, considering that Sam rarely ever *used* the dining table, and the paper had certainly not been there when she rushed by to leave for work that morning- In all her messes, she'd grown acutely aware of where any and every item in her home resided, no matter how many times it was moved in a rush, and no part of her day's mess included that piece of paper.

It was, without a doubt, not very normal at all.

With tired and withered hands, Sam reached for the paper, turning it over gingerly to find something scribbled across the other side, in handwriting that wasn't her own. Her eyes widened when she saw the writing- rushed, and with old, vintage ink that Sam remembered buying once on a whim- The fear melted into her veins, spreading and dissipating throughout her body like flecks of snow melting as soon as they landed.

The note read, with uneven and scratchy writing, *I am going to kill you.*

She looked up from the paper in a panic, meeting the slim, heterochromatic eyes of her cat staring back at her.

Turning, too quickly for her legs to keep from stumbling in her frightened state, Sam caught sight of her reflection in another mirror. There were far too many of them in the house, each one rusting and undeniably a bit creepy, but not bothersome enough to get rid of them, and now, her reflection was something entirely different.

The Sam in the mirror smiled. Not the tired, overworked, smile that Sam had grown accustomed to forcing through meetings, but something much more unnatural. Not quite her smile, but a poorly copied version, something inhuman.

I am going to kill you, the note had read.

This might have been the most abnormal thing of them all.

Sam yelped, and the noise almost sounded distorted when it reached her ears. Everything was moving too quickly, and she could feel her consciousness slipping from her like sand through the gaps of one's fingers, fast, falling, forgotten, until everything went black.

And yet, her body remained stable, standing still, even as she felt herself fading further and further away from it

That was incontrovertibly *not normal.*

Sam blinked, and it was then that she realized she was no longer in her body. She was watching, a few feet away from herself, through the mirror she had just seen herself in.

She called out for Damien, her voice finding it's way out in a horrible shriek. The cat did not move, only staring from far away at her body. Before long, she realized she couldn't see, her vision clouded by tears that threatened to choke her right then and there.

The other Sam smiled at the one in the mirror. It was that same, unsettling, shaky smile she'd seen before, when she was still in her body. It wasn't Sam. Her eyes flitted over her entire body- the version of her before her, and landed on a pair of freshy clean scissors. A family heirloom. Almost everything in the house was, and they were made with high-quality silvers and embellished with various designs so that they stood out. Up until today, they had never been used.

And so, with the grace of a woman much happier than Sam could ever have hoped to be, the other Sam used them.

Ladybugs by Tara Peterson

Potato Beetle by Tara Peterson

Their Village by Adactreus

Their village in which, a valley dips, a catacomb, of fear and wit, dined and doused of gold and gems, a tomb, a room of magic and

A young one, trapped, incarnate with fangs of bone, to seal his fate, legs as tall as god itself, too thin to walk on, no sense of self, the dust will rise and it will fall, from summer to spring, from winter to fall, it will sit and it will stay and it will clatter around, in this dismay and wait and eat what it can find, the rations of bugs and the scraps of its mind

And they will talk and they will say, do not go! Stay away! Horrors beneath you, this village is above that! he will loom in the dark with the bugs and the bats.

Years have passed, and it is known, that this thing has made their basement its home, and perhaps he will rise, normal, again

With the lift of a curse, and returning to man

But it will stay this way for quite a time, with thought for thought and rhyme for rhyme, and it will be quite a story of those whom will tell, but the boy's point of view it

Is
Not
Quite
As
Well.

What Is Love by Alistar Meier

PART 1

Where am I?
Alone. With me.
Am I real?
For now, yes; you are real.
Is this real?
Probably.
Who am I?
You are you.
Who does that make you?
Yours.

Why is it so dark?
Because the sun is mean.
Why is it mean?
It tried to take you from me.
Oh.
Don't talk about the sun.
Oh, okay.
Thank you.
Can I talk about the moon?
Maybe.

Where are you?
Here.
Where?
Right here.
I can't see you.
Hold on.
Okay.
Can you feel that?
Is that you?
Yes.

I need you.
Not right now.
Please?
I'm busy.
Please.
Why do you need me?
I don't know.
There must be some reason.
I don't know.
Fine.

PART 2

What is my name?
I don't know.
Do you have a name?
I don't know.
Then how do you know you are you?
Because I'm me.
And how do you know I am me?
Because.
Because why?
...
Hello?
Can you tell me something?
Of course. What is it?
Tell me a story.
What?
A story.
Oh. I will try.
Thank you.
...
Are you ok?
I am fine.
Can you not think of anything?
...
You are silly.

Being with you is nice.
Really?
Yes.

Why?
You are all I know.
That is not good.
It is when it's you.

You are my favorite.
What?
You heard me.
Oh.
I love you.
...

PART 3

What is your favorite color?
My favorite what?
Color.
What's that?
It's... color.
I don't know what that is.
What do you know?
Myself—
Only?
And you.

Your hair is soft.
Is it?
Yes, very.
Oh.
I like it.
Thank you.

Do you think we will ever see each other?
I don't know.
Yes you do. I can tell.
No you can't.
Yes I can.
...
Well?

PART 4

Do you know where we are?
...
Hello?
...
Where are you?
...
Hello?
...
HELLO?

Are you there?
...
I'll take that as a no.

I miss you.
...
I hope you are alive.

Revere by Jesse Liu

Evil Thoughts (excerpt) by Shi

Why is life like this
    Why is the public eye what it is
        Why does the government think they can choose who I am
Why
Just why
Why can't I be different
Why do I have to be the same as everyone else
Why can't I have my own opinion
 This world is is not good
This world is abusive
I would watch the world burn
I would let the world burn
In the words of Odysseus king of Ithaca I have had enough

Untitled by Ava Czygan

She was a ghostly figure of a woman, clad in white lace and skin so pale she was made of bone

She married Death itself, and at night her sheets were ice

Her hands raw and splattered like purple paint stains at their edges

She was never fond of living— rather, she boiled in tasteless melancholy and never spoke at length or with rhyme

Her tears so empty they evaporated before they reached her cheeks

But one day the sky shone too bright and burned her paper arms

Her body enveloped in heated orange and turned to ashy gray

Suddenly, her sheets thawed and her fingertips burst into flames

Her tears red hot continued falling and never stopped

Her bond with Death eternal,

Vanquished

And finally,

She lived

Shisif by Shi

The Island's Survivors by Charles Beaudry

I don't know how long we've walked for. It only felt like an hour, but we could've walked the entire day, for all I know. And yet, I still follow behind someone, like I've done my entire life. I guess I can't be that mad, though; he's the one who saved me from that cellar. Why should I try to lead us out of the dark if I can't understand what's happening on this island?

He looked back at me suddenly and said quietly, "Don't worry, we'll be there soon. Then, you'll be able to rest, okay?" It's like he can hear exactly what I'm thinking; it's freaky. I still don't trust him, but what other option do I have?

"Sure," I responded, feeling my legs pulse and my head spin from the humidity of walking through the forest. "Whatever you say."

He's a reserved person, or is at least quiet around me. He hasn't talked much on our trip to his destination. Then, he changed the direction in which he was walking through the forest, which caught my attention. I hadn't seen him change direction in so long that I wasn't used to him facing any other way. I wanted to say something, but I didn't at the time because I wasn't sure how exactly to feel about speaking up to him.

Suddenly, I felt anxious, almost claustrophobic, even when I gained freedom from that dark, crowded cellar. It was like I was walking back into the cell I was in. My brain started to fight my movements, and I felt my body freaking out, filling my mind with thoughts. Those thoughts weren't irrational to have, but at the same time, I didn't want to make things tense intentionally between us. Besides, he was the only one on this island who knew anything about it, so it felt as though I had to trust him.

"What are you doing?" He asked, the change in his tone of voice even more alarming to me.

"I don't believe you," I said, matching the sternness in his voice. I narrowed my eyes slightly and stood my ground. He stepped closer, his expression shifting into an irritated look.

"What do you mean?" He asked, still curious why my mood changed out of nowhere.

"I don't think what you're doing to help me involves your real intentions. I don't think there's some "safe haven" you've made on this god-forsaken island. I think you're lying to me."

"Why would I lie about something like that? I'm just trying to help you out. What's with the switch-up?"

"I'm just suspicious of you, which I think is very justified."

"I think you're just being unreasonable." At this point, I wanted to punch him for how smug he acted, like he knew everything.

"No, I'm being very reasonable! You somehow knew how to escape from that cellar. You make me follow you to a random place that you won't explain what or where it is. You make me follow you on a dark, shady path, and now you're saying I'm insane for being suspicious? Do you know how deranged you sound?" I saw his face change expressions as I argued with him, seeing him get angrier with every point I had brought up to him.

"You're only saying that because I haven't explained everything!" He's right, that's why I think he's faking it. He doesn't want to go into detail because there's probably nothing to explain, only that he's sided with the other freaks on this island.

"Exactly! Why won't you explain anything? Why are you so quiet?"

"Because I don't like to think about what I had to do."

"Why!? What did you have to do? Why do you say these things just to distract me from the fact that everything you've said has been a lie?"

"I'm not lying!" he shouted suddenly, almost a deafening scream to my ears. I felt my body jump, and I immediately listened to what he had to say. "We both were locked in the cellar, we both went through what you did!"

"...You both?"

"Yes. It was only me and a few others who survived after the plane crashed. We were captured and locked in that same cellar you were in. Luckily, we could escape only because a rescue team tried to help us, but they died saving us from those monsters. Chris and I were the only ones to survive that encounter. We ran into the forest, creating a shelter to hide in. A little home away from home. We planned how to escape the island and everything, we were going to come home. But then, they found us. They found us and burned everything we had. Then they grabbed Chris, and they started stabbing him, and all I did was run. I ran while I heard his screams and the cackling of fire all around me. The cheering grew louder around me as my best friend's screams ceased, and I can still hear those cheers as I walk through this forest. That's why I don't like talking about it, it hurts to remember. I was so stupid to leave him behind..."

Wow, I don't even know what to say to him. I wish he had admitted all this sooner, so I would believe everything he did for us. I didn't know...

He just started walking again after a minute, and I started walking behind him again. I didn't say anything after he explained his situation on the island. His sudden outburst shocked me so much that I had nothing else to say. All of the questions I had were answered, I guess.

Eventually, we ended up at his destination, a nice waterfall surrounded by forest and rock. There was nothing outside of the waterfall, only the animals and wildlife surrounding us in every direction. There seemed to be no other outside connection, just me and him in the middle of nowhere.

"Come on!" He exclaimed, seeming to light up at the thought of entering the waterfall. I followed him inside, and I was shocked to see he had made a decent living for himself whilst having close to nothing on this island. Obviously, it still didn't have much, but it was honest work he had put towards living on this island, and I respected that. It made me feel better about how much he's put towards surviving on this godforsaken island.

After a minute of looking around his makeshift home, I turned to him and smiled before saying, "Thank you for clarifying what you did to survive on this island. I couldn't trust you before, but now I feel like I can trust you with my life, with what you went through."

Looking around, I saw his face shift into a weird expression, a mix of relief and confusion. He spoke to me as if he were looking for an answer to his confusion. "Really? What does telling you what I've been through have to do with anything?" I looked back at him, listening to him as he asked his question. I breathe in before speaking again, my voice dropping slightly in volume.

"Because I never trust a survivor until I know what they've done to survive."

Souleater by Morgan DeVries

She's A maneater, make you work hard - **To be like her or else you'll never be respected in society, but if you try to be like her they will call you fake and unoriginal.**

Make you spend hard - **so now you are giving your money to the very companies who are destroying your self confidence.**

make you want all of her love

She's a maneater, make you buy cars

Make you cut cards.

wish you never ever met her at all- **because now there's a new trend and if you don't change everything again you will be ridiculed.**

Can't we just be how we want to be without society commenting about every little thing? You can't be too big or else you're a fat pig and you can't be too skinny or you're an attention seeker. Women can't even breathe without being judged. If you wear what you want to wear and not the latest trend you will be called emo or sloppy.

She's a souleater, a soul eater

(I been around the world, I ain't never meet a girl like this)
We've never been able to see everyone's opinion on something so easily. Social media is making beauty standards more unattainable and even more expected. If we can't even see ourselves as beautiful, how are we supposed to find the beauty in anything?

(I have been around the world, I ain't never met a girl like this) Nobody perfect exists, we put out how we want to be seen and then we are compared to how everyone else wants to be seen, so there is no girl that IS the beauty standard. Because you can **never** win.

Abstinence of Failure by Norhan Hassan

Strangers. All of us.
    Strange things happen all around us.
        They disturb us, surprise us, and concern us.
The odd thing is we all ask the wrong questions.

When god gave us the privilege of consciousness
The privilege of freedom, the privilege of choice.

Yet we can't be thankful.

We can't help but be vengeful.

Take that privilege from others
Take that privilege away from ourselves.

Free will

Hope

Humanity.

We tend to survive instead of live.
Breathing air isn't breathing unless you think about it.
You take your next breath without thinking; we tend to take that for granted.

Until we can't anymore,

We only look back and say I wish I lived.
I wish I had thought about taking that breath before taking my last.
But ignore what I said. You keep reading.

And I keep writing.

Keep looking down at the paper, keyboard, and step.
We look ahead,
but not really though..
We don't look ahead,
We just refuse to look back

Refuse to confront it, refuse to face it. In a way, we're running away from it.
At least I am, I know you are too.

When we write about happiness,
achievements,
college applications,
resumes.

We ignore what we can't do, how chained we are to our beliefs, and our limitations. Physically, and mentally, we have a choice. We crave it, then do it. Never can we quench it.

I can't help but fear
When I'm years into my life, to look back and wonder, what have I done
What have I wasted it on
Education, a job, money, family.

Notice how it was never me

Can't be you. You'll be selfish

Happiness is always judged
I'm always judged, so are you.

So when does it matter?
When it doesn't.

My parents say dont waste time
Time is like a sword, if you don't cut to it it'll cut you to it.
Time doesn't stop.
But we do.

60, 70, 80, 90.

Why do we do it?

We choose people.
Partners, friends, kids.
We surround ourselves with people, get hurt and repeat it.

Hoping for a change,

hoping for truth,

hoping for freedom.

The truth lies in front of us.

It will never happen.

It's always temporary.

It didn't happen when you were a kid.

It won't happen now.

It won't happen in the future.

We keep asking when, not how
We ask where is it but never look under us
Ask why but never look at the reason

We rewrite everything to fit our own narratives
Even if it wasnt true we trust it

A philosophy that sets us up for failure.

No matter how up the ladder you are,
How rich you are,
How successful,

how knowledgeable

You will still fail.

You will always fail.

Until you accept it.

The art of life.
You need to learn the rules before you break them.
You have to accept failure.
Embrace it.

We're so programmed to resenting,
fearing it,

yet we fear ourselves

We fear the failures we are,
 the failures they are,
the failures you are.

All of you.

But you specifically.

Have to embrace it

You have to fuck it up.
Not once,
not twice.
You'll mess it up all your life.
You might not ever get it right.

But you have to be conscious of that.

The privilege of failure,
We have that too.

Never forget that.

Eggs Are Nice by Alistar Meier

Eggs are nice.
    We're all just like eggs, y'know?
        Crack us all open and you can't tell one apart from another!
Right?
Actually, not really–
People aren't really like eggs, that was a stupid comparison.
But it's the same concept,
We all have the same blood!
I mean, not really...
Some people have a low red blood cell count,
Or *white* blood cell count,
Some people have had a blood transfusion,
Or heart transplant,
Or even an artificial heart to pump blood for them–
But we're still like eggs!
Kinda.
I mean, skin is like the shell;
There's different colors, sizes, shapes,
Some eggs even have a double yolk!
I'm not sure how that compares to humans,
But it's still cool!

Y'know,
The more I think about it,
Comparing humans to eggs isn't a great simile.
I mean, humans have complex thoughts and emotions–
Eggs just sit in a box in the fridge,
Wait to get cracked into a pan,
Or if they're lucky, get put into a casserole.
Humans don't get put into a casserole–
Unless you get eaten by a cannibal,
Or a really smart wolf.
Humans fall in and out of love,
Eggs don't feel anything.
Humans fight for what they think is right,
Eggs aren't strong enough to lift a sword.

Humans hurt each other,
Eggs...
Are just eggs.
That's why eggs are nice.

Prayers by Alicia Vargas Gonzalez

The sun has fallen, but light flashes across the endless nebula, swirls of violet and azure so vivid I could reach out and mold them with my fingers,

Carpet bunches around my scraped knees, sore elbows propped against the windowsill; hands clasped together in front of me.

It's a prayer, a prayer I have rehearsed since the sun came up, until it dipped below the mountains so far away.

I mimic what I've seen from the grown-ups all around me, imitating their sorry postures. Does your back hurt yet? Chin tilted down in reverence of something you've never had proof of,

But I'll pray,

I'll pray for large hands to not grab at my wrist, for a night I can hear the crickets chirping over the yelling, for my heart to stop twisting like a million knots.

Inclinations of hope hunger beneath my skin, reverberations of ramblings pushed through addled ears. How is this supposed to feel? Are my eyes supposed to open? Enlightenment bursting through my heart, my veins, my bones, seeping into every inch of skin exposed?

Is time slipping away? Like an opened wound, my hope gushes out; a depleted resource, why am I spending my time speaking to the stars when they're so far and bright they beg to be idolized; in the time we've spent looking for answers how many stars have burnt up that we've never even gotten the chance to admire?

The tragedies fold together like collapsing galaxies before my eyes, My hands slip down, my wish is gone, and just like that, the prayers gone wrong.

All Bark No Bite (excerpt) by Brooke Gordon

Life is tough when you have no teeth; Struggling to eat most food and being unable to hold my tongue inside my mouth when I sleep are just a few of my many hassles in life. Everyone's also constantly making fun of me for it, I can tell by the way they poke at my tongue when it hangs out.

My fur, which used to be a silky brown, is now balding in some areas. Whether it's because I'm old, or because of some unknown allergy, I don't know. However, what I do know is that I'm still as tough as I was in my prime.

People always just assume that I'm weak and pathetic. They hold this prejudice because all they see is a short, old dachshund called Weenie. Maybe if I was taller like a great dane, or scarier looking like a pitbull, they'd cower before me. But I'm not, and I've (mostly) accepted this.

As I've gotten older, none of my tactics seem to strike *fear* into people anymore. I don't know if it's the lack of teeth, or the bald spots, but *something* has to change if I want to stay the strong guard dog I once was.

DING DONG

The moment I hear that sound, a shock of thrill shoots through my body. *This is my chance.* I prepare my stumpy legs for takeoff, ready to bark and chase whoever dares to intrude in my house, and proceed to dart towards the door. As I get near, I sense something odd. *Another dog? Don't tell me...*

As I reach the entryway, I realize the tragedy that's about to unfold. A small, lanky dog is now being held in the arms of my owner. Her crusty, white fur shoots out from her body, making her resemble an old man. As her malicious, beady eyes lock onto mine, I can already tell her surprise visit is gonna be miserable.

Although she's a miniature, she still possesses the same satanic energy as a normal Jack Russell Terrier. So, though she might look harmless, my sister, Seamus, can do a lot more damage than one might think.

- - -

I used to live with a sweet, old couple when I was just a pup. Through much training, they raised me to be the smart, strong and brave dog that I am today. They passed along as much knowledge as they could before they passed away. So, a few months ago, I began living with one of their relatives.

This new owner, Ellen, feeds me a lot of treats, scratches me in spots I can't reach, and lets me sleep whenever and wherever I want, so I guess she's okay in my book. There's only one downside of living with her: the insane amount of people that trespass in her house.

Everytime that front door opens, I'm ready to protect Ellen. I don't discriminate based on age, gender, or even scent, I attack everyone who walks through that door *equally*. I will do whatever it takes to prove to her that my age and appearance don't matter: I will guard with my life.

However, this time it's not a person who I have to protect her from, it's my *sister*. And when I say sister, I'm not referring to a pup that came from the same mother, I'm referring to the demon of a dog I had to share my last home with.

I had to fight tooth and nail to get ANYTHING when she was around. That attention hog soaks up all the spotlight, making her owners fuss over her 24/7. It's truly no wonder she was given away so many times.

When our previous owners passed, a miracle happened: we were separated! Sent off to live with different relatives of our owners, I finally got some peace and quiet without all her yipping and yapping. However, every now and then, she still gets dumped on our doorstep to crash with us for a few days. Ellen calls it babysitting, I prefer to call it hell.

As Ellen carries my sister off to her bedroom, I can only glare. If I start the fight, it'll only make her look like an innocent victim. So instead, I do what anyone else would do in this situation, and I mark my territory right here on the floor. I'll make sure to prove to that hog who **really** belongs here.

- - -

I've often been told that I tend to overreact. Whether it's to the doorbell, or to how I bark at other dogs on walks (not that they don't deserve it, marking places that aren't theirs and all), I usually get told to take a chill pill.

Although with Seamus, everything she does deserves to be criticized. So, I'm gonna tell you three things about her so you can determine whether I'm overreacting about her surprise visit.

Number one: She's constantly butting in places she doesn't belong. In addition to the current example of her infiltrating my home, her favorite hobby is to snuggle up on *my* bed right as I leave the room. She then has the audacity to whine when I come back and perch myself on top of her.

Number two: She's hideous. Just plain hideous. I know I shouldn't be talking with my bald spots and all, but if you woke up and saw her in the middle of the night, you'd probably think a god just cursed you by dropping a giant, grotesque rat in the middle of your bed (talking from personal experience by the way).

Number three: I can't even stress this one enough, SHE'S AN ATTENTION HOG. From the moment you open your eyes, to the moment you're ready to fall asleep, she's there. Her clinginess makes every moment of your day worse than having a new-born child. So, for someone actually worthy of all the attention, guarding the house and all, I think you can understand that I am NOT overreacting when I say: this hog needs to get the hell out of my house.

- - -

I see you've made yourself comfortable, I glare at my sister from the end of the bed. Hopefully the bitter look in my eyes and the baring of my gums (again, no teeth) sent the message. It's only been a couple hours, but she's already getting on my nerves.

She's currently cuddled up against *my* owner, her raggedy fur smothered all around. Lifting her head, she looks over at me with her large, beady eyes. Her expression asking me *what are you gonna do about it?*

"I'm gonna go to the bathroom," Ellen suddenly exclaims, swinging her legs off the bed. "I'll be right back." As she starts towards the door, I watch as Seamus swiftly leaps off the bed. She acts as if left alone for two seconds, Ellen would just completely abandon us. Everyone, even my old self, knows they've only abandoned you once they're gone for over three minutes. *What an idiot.*

As I lay my head back down, a brilliant idea pops into my head. Slowly, I get up, stretch my back for a couple seconds, and casually stroll right over to Ellen's side of the bed. Plopping down directly against her pillow, I make myself comfy. *This is gonna be fun to watch.*

A couple minutes later, Ellen walks in with a glass of water in one hand, and Seamus in the other. She's easy to carry because she's all skin and bones—so light that a slight gust of wind is enough to knock her off her feet.

Finally noticing me, Ellen sighs and puts down her glass of water, "scootch, Weenie." Lightly shoving me aside, she's only able to push so much of me over with just a single arm. She quickly sets my sister on the other end of the bed and continues to push, and once she's satisfied with how much space she has, sits right back down. Though this time with a different dog cuddling next to her.

I'm delighted to look over and see the puzzled look on my sister's face, her eyes telling me that she seeks revenge. Her long, scrawny legs wobble over to the other side of the bed where our dog beds sit, and then proceeds to propel herself into *my* bed.

She has declared war, and I'm not the type of dog to back down.

Subspace by Claire Newell

The Night Air Is Screaming at Us

The night air is screaming at us. It has been for three hundred thousand and seven hundred fifty-five days straight. At least it would've been that many if we still had days. We didn't know at the time. We didn't know that they would vanish, but they have. All of them. It doesn't seem fair, you know? One just one, we only took one, and they all. They all, flee? Disappear? Abandon us? We don't completely know what happened. They're gone though that's the important part.

If only we had known what would happen we would have never done it. That's what we all say. Maybe it's even true. But in the moment, in the moment, we wouldn't have traded anything in the world for it. We knew that with all our hearts, we wouldn't have traded it for anything, the biggest oyster in the crystal sea, the livers of the stillborn gods, the desert of spices, nor a thousand other wonders, we boasted. But perhaps we would have traded it for salvation. Perhaps.

But the memories, the memories, are almost worth damnation. Almost. It was glorious, the hunt, the hunt that lasted Six hundred years. We chased it across the sky, beyond the sky, into the dark abyss. We feared we'd never catch it. But we did. We reached it, we attacked it, our battle echoed across the cosmos. We died in droves, but it did not matter because there were always more of us. Back home we were dying to die. Dying to contribute to the war effort(for it had grown from a hunt to an all-consuming war)in any way we could. We murdered each other for spots on the ships. We put our unborn children on the waiting lists for elite training. The ashes of our fallen grew so numerous that they formed rings around our planet. Victory was a forgone conclusion for we could die a million deaths, and a million more would clamor to take their place, our foe could only die once. And die it did, with our strong encouragement of course. Bathed in light and glory we dragged the corpse home to claim the spoils of our victory.

Then the feast came. The feast! The wondrous feast! Just the memories of it make our mouths water and our bellies groan. We ate and ate for its flesh was so wondrous that after we had tasted it all other food was ash, and every moment not indulging in it was so empty in comparison that it became painful. As we feasted, as heaven passed through our lips, as we glowed with joy, we felt such pleasure that we could just die with no regrets. Now we wish we had. Now we have only the memories. The bittersweet memories, like faded gold or honeyed poison. They are all we have. They are what we gave up everything for. Some of us say they really were worth it. It's a comforting lie or a grim truth.

"What was it like, before, when they were here?" They ask

It is them who are the most betrayed. Those too young to have known the light, too young to have feasted on sin. Too young to have known when the night was silent, when the surface was warm. They are the heirs to our cold dead world, even though they had no hand in its murder

"It, it was…"

We hesitate, we always do, every time they ask. They have asked us all, the few who are left. We have never given them the full answer. What good would it do? To tell them of things they will never have, to give them nostalgia for memories that aren't theirs, to cut a hole in their hearts and fill it with the absence of light we say this to ourselves. But we know that that isn't the only reason. We fear that they will hate us. That they will curse us and spit venom at us. That we will know deep down that they are right, that we won't resist when they throw us out of these caves and into the screaming night. Some part of us wants to tell them, wants to be punished, to be abandoned. This part thinks that it can bear the fury and rejection of our children more than it can bear the pain of keeping them in the dark. The part that wants to submit. Submit to the judgment of our children, of ourselves, of the night. The other part wants to live. It wants to curl itself in a little ball and wrap our memories around itself like a blanket. It wants to regain our strength and lead us on another glorious campaign, to meet the night's screams with our war cries. It wants to finish what we started, to hunt every last one down and leave the world in total darkness. Another part wants to forget, forget the light, forget the warmth, forget the war, it wants to bury the past under a thousand miles of voidstone and build. Build a world for the future, for our children, our betrayed children.

"It was" (Glorious, terrible, none of your concern, warm, harsh, impossible)

"Different" (we shall let them come to their own conclusions we compromise)

"We used to be able to go to the surface. We actually lived up there"

"And the surface, what was it like?" They ask right on cue

"About half the time, depending on the season, it was warm and bright. We called that day."

"The other half was darker but there were still lights, small lights like sparks, or embers. We called that night, but it wasn't the same as this night"

"What is it like now, why can't we go to the surface now?" There is genuine curiosity in their voices but also some resignation like they doubt we will answer truthfully.

No more! No longer! We cannot bear to keep them in the dark for another second.

"It's hell. Up above is hell. Down here it's safe, it's not heaven but it's safe."

"Why, what's up there?"

"There is nothing up there, nothing but the moonless, starless, empty night. That terrible eternal night, that screams and shrieks as if its heart has been ripped out."

"What does it sound like?" They are getting excited now; even if they think it's a lie it's a new one at least.

"It sounds like every hair on your body being blown off a mile below the surface, like your ears dripping with red and a web of cracks across your horns half a mile below, and the surface. At the surface it sounds like steam hissing as your eyes sizzle, your blood boils, and your skin charrs." It is a scream of grief, and rage so pure and overwhelming that it is as if all other grief was a pale imitation of it."

"Why, is the night screaming why is she so sad and mad?"

We steel ourselves," The night air is screaming at us bec-"

"She's screaming at us? What did we do to her? What did you do to her"? they interrupt yelling questions over each other.

We clear our throat and they all fall silent

"The night air is screaming at us because we have eaten the sun"

Beauty in Plain Sight by Charles Beaudry

Dead Men by Adactreus

A shining star, glimmering light cacophony of wispy flight—
But we shall never reach them.
They float too far, a perilous plight, illumination far too bright, a hope- a dream, a fleeting thought, a thing to hold, but what is naught– not what we think but what we know, an iridescent glow–
But we shall never have them.
We will work and we will stay *on the ground*, to our dismay,
And yet we're not redeemed.
The ones above us far too clever, our wants deceived and warped.
Eternity says, we will live forever, for dead men tell no secrets.

What It Means To Be Human by Tejasvi Annadurai

To be human
    is to forget what you walked into a room for
    and laugh at yourself out loud.
It's spilling coffee on your shirt
right before something important
and deciding,
"Well, I'm interesting now."

It's singing in the shower
like you're the headliner of a world tour.
It's dancing badly in your socks
when no one's home—
or even better, when someone is.

To be human
is to feel everything.
All at once.
To cry during commercials.
To get goosebumps from a song you've heard a thousand times.
To get hit by a smell that time-travels you back to your grandmother's kitchen,
or your first day of school,
or a hug you didn't know you still remembered.

It's not always knowing what you're doing—
but doing it anyway.
Winging it.
Tripping through conversations,
saying the wrong thing,
fixing it with a smile and a "Wait—what I meant was..."
and trying again.

To be human
is to laugh until your stomach hurts.

To snort when you laugh
and own it.
It's inside jokes and second chances,
bad puns and shared playlists.
It's friendships built out of "you too?"
and "I thought I was the only one."

It's having big, wild dreams
and chasing them in sneakers with holes in the toes.
It's falling, sometimes,
but also flying.
It's the magic of realizing you've grown—
that something that used to shake you
doesn't anymore.

It's change.
So much change.
So much becoming.
And it's good.

To be human
is to forget birthdays
and remember kindness.
It's writing things in your notes app at 2 a.m.
that feel like poetry,
even if they're just fragments.
It's saying "I love you" first
or saying nothing
but meaning everything
with a look, a laugh, a touch.

To be human
is potential.
Pure, radiant potential.
You are allowed to reinvent yourself.
To try, fail, pivot,
restart.
You are allowed to take up space.
To get it wrong.
To learn.
To grow.

To glow.

You are allowed to feel joy without guilt.
To let things be good.
To sit in the sunlight and let the warmth say,
you don't always have to be striving.
You can just be.

To be human
is to be a walking canvas,
always unfinished,
always beautiful.
It's messy, vibrant, unpredictable—
but alive.
And that aliveness?
That's the gift.

You are stardust with a heartbeat.
Electricity in motion.
Possibility in a hoodie.

You are every laugh that makes someone breathe easier.
Every goofy dance in a kitchen.
Every spark of "what if?"
and "maybe I could."

What it means to be human
is that you get to try.
You get to feel.
You get to make a mess
and call it art.

You get to live.
Fully.
Boldly.
Brilliantly.
Exactly as you are.

www.ingramcontent.com/pod-product-compliance
Lightning Source LLC
LaVergne TN
LVHW022001060526
838201LV00048B/1650